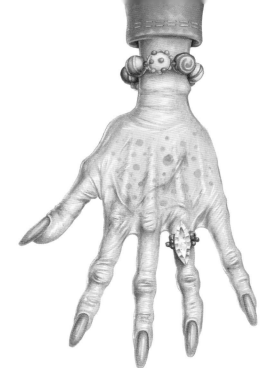

Nana's Getting Married

Heather Hartt-Sussman

Illustrated by **Georgia Graham**

TUNDRA BOOKS

Published in Canada by Tundra Books,
75 Sherbourne Street, Toronto, Ontario M5A 2P9

Published in the United States by Tundra Books of Northern New York,
P.O. Box 1030, Plattsburgh, New York 12901

Library of Congress Control Number: 2009928989

Design: Jennifer Lum
Printed in China

Library and Archives Canada Cataloguing in Publication

Hartt-Sussman, Heather
    Nana's getting married / Heather Hartt-Sussman ; illustrated by
Georgia Graham.

ISBN 978-0-88776-911-5

I. Graham, Georgia, 1959- II. Title.

PS8615.A757N36 2010   JC813'.6   C2009-902835-2

We acknowledge the financial support of the Government of Canada
through the Book Publishing Industry Development Program (BPIDP)
and that of the Government of Ontario through the Ontario Media
Development Corporation's Ontario Book Initiative.
We further acknowledge the support of the Canada Council for
the Arts and the Ontario Arts Council for our publishing program.

ONTARIO ARTS COUNCIL
CONSEIL DES ARTS DE L'ONTARIO

Medium: chalk pastels and chalk pastel pencils on sanded paper; chalk
pastels and chalk pastel pencils on cold press illustration board

1 2 3 4 5 6   15 14 13 12 11 10

For Scotty and Jack
And to Sir, with Love
– H.H.S.

For Grandpa and Nell
– G.G.

Nana was the best grandma in the world, until she met Bob.

She baked me chewy chocolate chip cookies and let me eat the dough. She knitted me mittens and socks and turtleneck sweaters with snowflakes on them. She told me stories at bedtime that always had happy endings.

But ever since she met Bob, every-thing has changed.

Now Nana does her hair differently. She gets pedicures on Friday afternoons. And instead of staying home with me on weekends, she goes out with her boyfriend, Bob.

I, for one, do not approve.

My parents seem happy for her. Mom helps pick out what she'll wear on her dates. Dad tells her about a terrific new show playing nearby. And they send her off with a wave and a smile, telling her she looks great.

I don't think she looks great. I think the clothes Mom picks out for her are dreadful, not to mention inappropriate. The thought of Bob holding her hand at the show makes me want to gag.

"Nana sure looks amazing," says Mom.

"Gross,"
I say.

N ow Nana takes up hours and hours
in the bathroom having bubble baths.

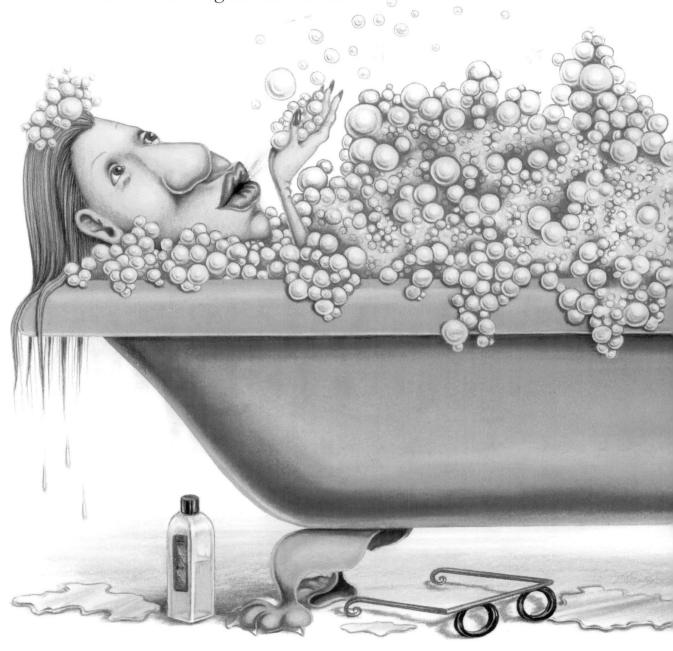

"When Nana stops dating Bob, can I have the bathtub all
to myself like before?" I ask.

"Nana just needs to freshen up for her date," says Mom.

"And it doesn't look like she's going to stop seeing Bob anytime soon," says Dad.

I think Dad is right because Nana keeps pictures of Bob by her bedside. She sings silly love songs to herself all day long. She even puts on makeup!

When Nana won't get off the phone, I pick up the receiver and loudly clear my throat. But she never seems to get the hint.

"After Bob goes away, can I have Nana all to myself like before?" I ask.

"It looks like Bob is here to stay," says Mom.

"I think Nana's in love," says Dad.

"Isn't that wonderful?" they say.

"Gross," I say.

"You have friends," says Mom, "so why
can't Nana have a special friend too?"

*Yeah, but I don't spray perfume all over the
place every time Ricky and Matthew come over.*

"You talk to your friends privately, without interruption," says Dad, "so why can't Nana have a little privacy too?"

Yeah, but I don't call my friends silly baby names, like Snoocums and Honey Bunch, or giggle like a chipmunk when I talk to them on the phone.

My parents know

I do not approve.

I've tried everything – pretending I am sick so she'll make me chicken soup with rice; pretending I'm afraid of a lightning storm so she'll stay home, instead of going out for dinner and dancing. Once, I even tried to scare Bob away.

Sometimes I am so naughty, my parents have to send me to my room.

But no matter what they do,

I still do not approve.

Before you know it, things get even worse. Mom shows Nana the latest exercise craze. Dad suggests they double-date. So Mom and Dad and Nana and Bob all go out and leave me at home with a sitter!

"Your grandma sure looks pretty," says the sitter.

"Gross," I say.

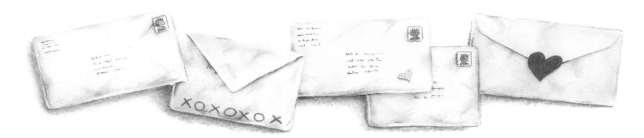

Mom and Dad think it's cute when Nana gets love letters in the mail. They think it's funny when Nana burns her bread in the toaster because she's too busy daydreaming about Bob. They think it's sweet when Nana and Bob share a soda pop out of the very same glass with two straws.

"Isn't that absolutely adorable?" they say.

I, for one, do not approve.

One evening, when Bob comes over to take Nana out, I know she isn't quite ready. So I ask him to sit in the den with me. I tell him all about Nana's arthritis and her bad knee and the gallstones she had removed three years ago. I talk about her memory, which is not as good as it used to be.

"I know all about her knee, her gallstones, and her memory," says Bob. "Some of my parts don't work so well anymore either. But for me, your nana is perfect. And I think I'm perfect for her too."

I, for one, am not so sure.

But when she comes downstairs, everyone says how lively she looks.

"Nana sure looks bubbly," says Mom.

"Gross," I say.

I tell my friends to enjoy their grandmas while they can. "Let them give you big wet kisses. Let them make sappy speeches about the day you were born. Let them pinch your cheeks and part your hair on the wrong side," I say. "They might meet a man like Bob and all that could change. They could start acting all weird!"

I've tried everything – going on strike (no one noticed); running away (it started to snow);

stamping and **pouting** and **whining** and **sulking**.

Nothing works. Bob keeps coming back for Nana.

And I, for one, do not approve.

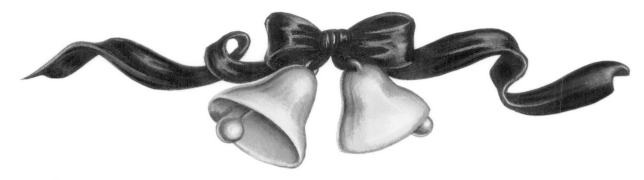

One day Nana sits me down and tells me she and Bob are planning a wedding. "And I want you to be the ring bearer," she says.

"No way," I say. "Why should I? You don't bake me chewy chocolate chip cookies and let me eat the dough anymore. You don't knit anything – no mittens or socks or turtleneck sweaters with snowflakes on them. You don't tell as many bedtime stories with happy endings. And," I say, "I don't like Bob."

Nana rocks me gently in her arms and tells me that after she and Bob get married, they'll be moving just a couple of streets away. "It doesn't mean I'll forget about you," she says. "We'll just have a new member in the family. And," she adds, "Bob is hoping you can spend weekends with us sometimes."

"Bob said that?" I ask.

"Yup," says Nana. "He's even building a tree house for you in the backyard."

"He is?" I ask.

"Uh-huh," says Nana, rocking me some more. "Sweetie, Bob makes me happy. He's perfect for me and I think I'm perfect for him. I'm sure you'd like him, if you just give him a chance."

Nana's eyes glow like brand-new marbles held up to the light. "She sure looks happy," I say to myself.

At the wedding, I carry the rings proudly. Mom arranges Nana's bouquet, and Dad seats the guests.

Then the bride appears. Everyone starts to whisper.

"Imagine, at her age!" one woman says.

"She's blushing like a teenage girl," says another.

"I think Nana looks beautiful,"

I say, loud enough for everyone to hear.

When the judge asks if anyone objects to the marriage, Bob turns
and gives me a big wink.

I don't know about anyone else,

but I, for one, approve.